SAMANTHA'S BLUE BICYCLE

SAMANTHA · 1904

BY VALERIE TRIPP

ILLUSTRATIONS DAN ANDREASEN

VIGNETTES PHILIP HOOD, SUSAN MCALILEY

THE AMERICAN GIRLS COLLECTION®

Published by Pleasant Company Publications
Previously published in *American Girl*® magazine
Copyright © 2002 by Pleasant Company
For information, address: Book Editor, Pleasant Company Publications,
8400 Fairway Place, P.O. Box 620998, Middleton, WI 53562.

Visit our Web site at **americangirl.com**

Printed in Singapore.
02 03 04 05 06 07 08 09 TWP 10 9 8 7 6 5 4 3 2 1

Library of Congress Cataloging-in-Publication Data

Tripp, Valerie, 1951–
Samantha's blue bicycle / by Valerie Tripp ;
illustrations, Dan Andreasen ; vignettes, Philip Hood, Susan McAliley.
p. cm. — (The American girls collection)
Summary: In 1905, when nine-year-old Samantha has trouble
riding her new bicycle, her grandmother offers a surprising solution.
Includes notes on the history of bicycles and bicycling.

ISBN 1-58485-481-2
[1. Bicycles and bicycling—Fiction. 2. Grandmothers—Fiction.
3. Clothing and dress—Fiction.] I. Andreasen, Dan, ill.
II. Hood, Philip, ill. III. McAliley, Susan, ill. IV. Title. V. Series.
PZ7.T7363Sao 2002   [Fic]—dc21   2001036377

The
AMERICAN GIRLS
COLLECTION™

OTHER AMERICAN GIRLS
SHORT STORIES:

PICTURE CREDITS

The following individuals and organizations have generously given permission to reprint illustrations contained in "Looking Back": p. 30—National Cycle Museum of Wales; p. 31—Ordinary, GV3.81/p3, Photo by *Minneapolis Journal*, Minnesota Historical Society; Safety bike, Poster Collection, Zurich Museum of Design; p. 32—Culver Pictures; p. 33—Courtesy of the Valentine Museum, photo by Dane Penland, Division of Printing and Photographic Services, Smithsonian Institution; p. 34—Wisconsin Historical Society WHS 1967.275; p. 35—Wisconsin Historical Society WHI (X3)53986; pp. 36–37—Pryor Dodge Collection; p. 38—Reprinted by permission Random House Archive and Library, Rushden, UK; p. 39—*The Pneumatic*, Nov. 1898; p. 40—Photography by Jamie Young.

TABLE OF CONTENTS

SAMANTHA'S FAMILY
AND FRIENDS

SAMANTHA'S FAMILY

GRANDMARY
*Samantha's grandmother,
who wants her to be
a young lady.*

UNCLE GARD
*Samantha's favorite uncle,
who calls her Sam.*

SAMANTHA
*A nine-year-old orphan
who lives with her wealthy
grandmother.*

AUNT CORNELIA
*An old-fashioned beauty who
has newfangled ideas.*

AGNES & AGATHA
*Samantha's newest
friends, who are
Cornelia's sisters.*

SAMANTHA'S
BLUE BICYCLE

Grandmary!" Samantha called out excitedly. "It's Uncle Gard and Aunt Cornelia! They're here!"

Down the stairs Samantha flew, and out the big doors to the front porch. She took the steps in a single leap and threw herself into Gard's arms just as he climbed out of his auto. "Oh, Uncle Gard!" she said. "We missed you so!"

"We missed you too, Sam," said Gard as he hugged her. "We're glad to be back."

This was Gard and Cornelia's first visit to Mount Bedford since their wedding. After their honeymoon they  had taken a few days to settle into their new town house in New York City. Samantha had been waiting impatiently for this visit. She wanted it to be perfect, so Gard and Cornelia would come visit often. She did not want to be left out of their lives now that they were married.

Grandmary came down the steps and hugged Cornelia hello. Then she tilted her cheek to receive Gard's kiss. "Gardner, dear," she said. "It has been entirely too dull and quiet here without you and your dreadful automobile."

Cornelia smiled at Samantha. "What a pretty pinafore!" she said. "Is it new?"

"Yes," said Samantha happily. She held out the skirt of the ruffly white pinafore. "It's special for your visit."

"It makes you look very tall," said Cornelia. "I believe you've grown a foot since we've been away."

Gard stared at Samantha's feet. "Still only two that I can see," he joked. "Thank goodness! Otherwise she'd have a hard time using the present we brought her." With a dramatic *whoosh*, Gard pulled the canvas tarp off the back of the auto. Samantha gasped when she saw what was there: three shiny new bicycles.

"We got them in England," said Gard

as he lifted the bicycles down. "They're the very latest models."

"I told Gard it was high time you had a bicycle, Samantha," said Cornelia. "I loved cycling when I was your age. It's so fast and free! I'm sure you'll love it, too."

"And here's the best part of all," added Gard. "We're going to leave the bicycles here in Mount Bedford. Just think of the fun we'll have, the three of us, bicycling together!"

The three of us . . . Samantha was so happy she couldn't speak.

"This one is yours, Sam," said Gard. He rolled a beautiful blue bicycle toward her.

"Oh, thank you," said Samantha. She

put one hand on the shiny handlebars and the other on the leather seat and looked up at her grandmother. "Please, Grandmary," she asked eagerly, "may I keep it?" She was worried, for she knew very well that Grandmary thought bicycles were dangerous and not quite proper for young ladies. That's why Samantha had never had one, even though she was nine years old.

Grandmary sighed. "In my day," she said, "bicycles were ridden in circus acts by women wearing tights. Soon everywhere you looked there were women riding bicycles on the streets. Some of them wore hideous short, puffy trousers called bloomers. We referred to those women as Bloomer

Girls." She sniffed. "Most unladylike!"

Cornelia spoke up gently. "A lady is a lady no matter what she's wearing," she said. "I hardly think Samantha will act improperly on her bicycle."

"Indeed not!" Grandmary replied tartly. She turned and smiled at Samantha. "I can see that you have your heart set on riding this bicycle with Gard and Cornelia, dear girl," she said. "You may keep it if you promise to be careful."

"I will," promised Samantha.

"Well then, hop on, Sam!" said Gard. He held the bike. When Samantha sat on the seat, the skirt of her dress and her pinafore and her petticoats billowed around her. She tucked them all under her legs to get them out of the way. Then Gard pushed and she pedaled and the wheels turned, and there she was, riding the bicycle with Gard running alongside, holding her steady!

"Hurray!" Cornelia cheered.

The ruffles on Samantha's pinafore fluttered, and her heart did, too. Riding the bicycle was harder than she had thought it would be. She tried to keep the front tire from wobbling, and she tried to keep a smile on her face, but she was nervous. She was afraid she would topple over if it were not for Gard's firm hold.

"Are you ready for me to let go?" Gard asked after a few minutes.

Samantha gulped. "Yes," she said,

*There she was, riding the bicycle with Gard
running alongside, holding her steady!*

wanting to impress Gard and Cornelia by being a quick learner. Gard let go, and she rode the bike in a big, slow, shaky circle on the driveway.

When she stopped, Gard and Cornelia clapped and cheered. "I knew you'd get the hang of it right away!" Cornelia praised her.

"Let's go to the park," Gard suggested with enthusiasm. "There are lots of paths there, so you won't have to go round in circles."

"Dear me!" said Grandmary. "Don't you think it's a bit too soon?"

"I think it's up to Sam," said Gard. "If she's plucky enough to try the park, then we should let her. What do you say, Sam?"

Samantha was *not* sure she wanted to go to the park, but she *was* sure she wanted to be plucky. "Let's go," she said.

"That's my girl!" said Gard proudly.

༄

The park was crowded with bicyclists enjoying the sunny spring day. Samantha thought they were all cycling rather fast, as if their bicycles were being hurried along by the brisk spring breeze.

"Be careful," Grandmary cautioned from her perch on a park bench. "Don't go too fast."

"You go first, Sam," said Gard as they wheeled their bicycles to the path that ran alongside the lake. "Cornelia and I will follow and keep an eye on you."

"All right," said Samantha. Feeling awkward and unsteady, she mounted her bicycle. She wanted to tuck her skirts out of the way, but there wasn't time. Her bicycle started rolling forward before she had even pushed down on the pedals!

The path was wide, but it wasn't as flat or as smooth as the driveway. It dropped off sharply on her right along the bank of the lake. Samantha pedaled slowly, concentrating as hard as she could on not falling.

Suddenly she felt a tug. She looked down. Her skirt had caught in the bike chain! She started to yank it free, but just then Uncle Gard shouted, "Watch out!"

Samantha looked up. To her horror, she saw that a cyclist was flying straight toward her at top speed! In a panic, Samantha swerved hard to the right. Her bike lurched off the path and bounced down the bank, out of control.

"Help!" she shrieked. She struggled to steer, but the front wheel wobbled violently. *Crash!* The bicycle smashed into a huge rock. In a terrible tangle, Samantha and the bicycle fell right into the mucky water at the edge of the lake. *Splash!*

"Samantha!" shouted Gard and Cornelia as they rushed down the slope to help her. "Are you all right?"

Samantha bit her lip and nodded,

*Samantha looked up. To her horror, she saw that
a cyclist was flying straight toward her at top speed!*

though she was fighting back tears. Her ankle was twisted, her stockings torn, and she had a bad scrape on one hand. Her new pinafore was mud-spattered, grass-stained, and grease-streaked. Her skirt was so badly twisted around the chain that she had to rip it to get it free.

Grandmary appeared at the top of the bank. "Merciful heavens!" she exclaimed. "It's a wonder you weren't killed! I hope no bones are broken."

"No, Mother," Gard called up to her as he helped Samantha stand. "Sam's fine."

"The poor child's had enough foolishness for one day," said Grandmary firmly. "We're going home—right now."

When Grandmary said *poor child,*

Cornelia got a stubborn look in her eye. "Samantha," she asked, "do you want to go home now?"

With all her heart, Samantha wanted to go home. She hated the idea of getting back on the bicycle. But she hated the idea of disappointing Gard and Cornelia even more. She wiped her hands on her ruined pinafore and tried to think what to say.

"Got to get back on the horse that threw you, right, Sam?" said Uncle Gard.

Samantha looked at the muddy bicycle and noticed something. With tremendous relief she said, "I don't think I *can* get back on, Uncle Gard. The front tire is flat."

Gard picked up

the bicycle and looked at the tire. "You're right," he said. "We'll have to have it fixed. No more riding today."

"What a shame!" said Cornelia with a sigh.

"Don't be too disappointed, Sam," Gard said as they walked back to the automobile. "We'll try again soon. Meanwhile, you'll have time to practice."

Practice? thought Samantha. *I never want to get on that bicycle again as long as I live!*

❧

One afternoon a few days later, when Samantha came home from school, Grandmary said, "Hawkins has fixed your bicycle."

"That's nice," said Samantha dully.

"He will help you if you feel you must practice," Grandmary added.

"*No!*" said Samantha. "I mean, no thank you, not today. I can't! I . . . I have too much schoolwork to do."

"Very well," said Grandmary.

Samantha could tell by the look on Grandmary's face that she was a little surprised. She wished she could tell Grandmary how fearful she was of the bicycle, but she was too ashamed of her fear to tell the truth.

For the next week, whenever Samantha walked past the carriage house, she looked away, thinking about the bicycle sitting inside unused. Whenever she remembered her scary fall, she shivered. She wished she *had* broken some bones. She wished she had damaged the bicycle beyond all repair. She wished she'd get the chicken pox again, or that winter would come back and cover everything with snow. Anything, *anything* to excuse her from riding that hateful bicycle.

Then, on Saturday afternoon, the telephone rang.

"Hello!" said Gard's cheery voice. "Guess what? Cornelia and I are coming out to Mount Bedford next weekend, and we're bringing Cornelia's sisters with us. Agnes and Agatha are crackerjack cyclists. We'll all go on a long bicycle ride together and bring a picnic. Doesn't that sound like fun, Sam?"

"Mmm-hmm," said Samantha, her heart sinking.

"Keep practicing," said Gard. "See you soon! Good-bye!"

"Good-bye," said Samantha. After she hung up the telephone, she stood next to it for a moment, deep in misery. She pictured herself standing with Grandmary on the front porch, waving good-bye to Gard, Cornelia, Agnes, and Agatha as they tootled off merrily on their bicycles, leaving her behind. How could she tell Gard and Cornelia that she hated the bicycle they'd given her and that they'd *never* ride together again?

In desperation, Samantha went to the carriage house. She wheeled her bicycle out onto the driveway and climbed on nervously. She took a deep breath, pushed down on one pedal, and rolled forward. Just as before, the front tire wobbled  wildly, her skirt got caught in the chain, and *crash!* Down she fell on the driveway.

"I can't do it! I can't!" she wailed to no one. She pulled her skirt free, kicked the bike away from her in anger, then bent her head and cried in shame and frustration.

Grandmary came out of the house. She knelt next to Samantha and put her arms around her. She let Samantha finish crying before she asked, "Are you all right, dear?"

"I hate that bicycle!" Samantha said fiercely. "I'm scared to ride it. Every time I do, my skirt gets tangled, I lose control, and I fall. Uncle Gard said I was plucky, but I'm not. I'm a scaredy-cat."

"And yet you tried again just now," said Grandmary. "I saw you."

Samantha tried to explain. "Riding bicycles was something Uncle Gard and Aunt Cornelia and I were going to do *together*," she said slowly. "If I can't ride, I'm afraid they won't visit very often . . ."

"And we'll be left out of their lives," Grandmary finished for her.

Samantha nodded.

"Well," said Grandmary, "perhaps I can help you."

Samantha was surprised. "But I thought you didn't approve of the bicycle," she said. "I thought you didn't want me to ride it."

Grandmary smiled. "I would not have chosen a bicycle for you myself," she said. "But I don't want you to be left out of the fun. Besides, it's you who'll have to ride the bicycle, not I. Do you think you can do it?"

Samantha took a deep breath. She looked at the bicycle, then she looked at Grandmary. "I really want to try," she said.

"Very well," said Grandmary. "Here's what we'll do . . ."

❧

Saturday was bright and beautiful.

"It's just the day for a bike ride!" exclaimed Gard as he helped Cornelia, Agnes, and Agatha out of the auto at Grandmary's house.

"Indeed it is," said Grandmary, coming down the steps to greet them.

Samantha opened her window and called, "Hello, everyone!"

"Hello, Sam!" Uncle Gard called back. "Are you ready for some fun?"

"I sure am!" answered Samantha. "I'll be right there!" When Samantha burst out of the front doors, all of the visitors gasped.

"Jiminy!" exclaimed Agnes. "Bloomers!"

"Bloomers!" Agatha sighed enviously. "Samantha, you're so lucky! I can't believe Grandmary lets you wear them."

"They were Grandmary's idea!" said Samantha. "Now I don't have to worry

about my skirt getting caught. I've been
wearing bloomers all week while I've
practiced riding. Watch this!"

Samantha hopped on her bicycle and
rode in a big circle around the driveway
without wobbling a bit.

"Why, Grandmary," said Cornelia.
"You astonish me."

Grandmary's eyes twinkled. "A lady is a lady no matter what she's wearing," she said. Then she and Cornelia laughed together.

"Come on, everyone," called Samantha. "Let's go!" Samantha led the way on her beautiful blue bicycle. At the end of the driveway, she turned and waved good-bye to Grandmary. Then she rode off down the road.

"Hey, Sam!" Uncle Gard called after her. "Wait for us!"

VALERIE TRIPP

At 9   *Now*

Atter I crashed into a rock and had a terrible fall, I feared and hated my bicycle just as Samantha did. But I hated even more being left behind when my sisters went on long bike rides. Training wheels— not bloomers—helped me overcome my fear and learn to love bike riding.

Valerie Tripp has written forty-four books in The American Girls Collection, including seven about Samantha

A Peek Into
the Past

When Samantha was growing up in the
early 1900s, bicycling was a popular pastime
for everyone, including women and girls.
But it had taken bicycle inventors many tries
before they discovered a design that was
easy and safe for women and girls to ride.

Some of the earliest bicycles had big
wooden wheels with iron tires.
These bicycles were called
boneshakers because they
were such a bumpy
ride! Later, in the
1880s, bicycles with
huge front wheels

A boneshaker

were designed. The "high-wheeler" became so popular that people began to call it the *ordinary*. But riding the ordinary took skill and balance, and wearing a skirt made it almost impossible.

By the early 1890s, the *safety bike* had been invented. It was the first bike that women and girls could ride easily. The bike had enclosed gears that kept skirts from getting tangled in the chains. The safety bike also had two equal-sized

A safety bike

wheels and a dropped frame with no crossbar. In 1898, the coaster brake was added to the safety bike. To use this brake, the rider pushed the pedal back to make the bicycle stop. All of these features made riding the safety bike a breeze!

To make riding even easier, many women and girls also changed their style of clothing. They started wearing *bloomers,* or full pants gathered at the knee.

A "Bloomer Girl"

When people first saw women in bloomers, they were flabbergasted. Many people did not think that bloomers were appropriate clothing for women. But women and girls continued to wear them. By 1895, "Bloomer Girls" were a common sight in American cities.

Soon people accepted this change, and clothes that fit more active lifestyles became fashionable. Women began wearing shorter skirts and split skirts. Cycling skirts were often brown or tan—a proper young lady wouldn't want the dust and dirt to show! Tight-fitting corsets made it difficult for women to breathe

A split skirt

A health corset

while bicycling, so the *health corset* or *bicycle waist* became popular. This corset had a straight front, so it did not press on a woman's abdomen when she was riding.

In the 1890s, a bicycling craze swept America. Everyone was cycling, and towns formed cycling clubs. The Metropolitan Academy in New York City set aside an area for women to learn to bicycle. In the winter, men and women attended "musical rides," where they pedaled in circles to the music of a live orchestra.

Indoor bicycling clubs allowed people to ride their bicycles year round.

35

Another popular New York City club was the *Michaux* (mee-show) Club. It was named after Pierre Michaux, a Frenchman who manufactured one of the first two-wheeled bicycles. The Michaux Club began in 1895 as a place for people to ride in the winter. Men and women had separate riding sessions. In the morning, women received their riding lessons. After lunch, they rode to music and enjoyed tea served in the clubrooms. Women also took part in "ten-pin rides,"

where they demonstrated their skills by riding their bicycles in and out of a line of bowling pins.

Riders also showed off their skills in *gymkhana* (jim-KAH-nuh) festivals—a new craze from India. The bicyclists wore elaborate red and white uniforms and rode bicycles decorated with red and white ribbons. The festival was full of activities to do on bicycles, such as relay races, fancy-riding exhibitions, and a grand march. At the end of the evening, men and women "danced" the Virginia Reel on their bicycles.

These European ads show how popular gymkhana festivals were overseas, too.

Many couples thought the bicycle was romantic. They went for bicycle rides together or rode *tandem* bicycles, which were built for two riders. One young woman even rode off on the family tandem to elope with her young gentleman!

A tandem wedding

For many women, the bicycle was a "freedom machine." Before bicycles, people used horses to get around. Girls weren't usually allowed to drive or ride horses by themselves. But bicycles easily took a girl almost anywhere she wanted to go.

Not everyone thought this new freedom machine was a good thing. The writer of this poem certainly didn't!

Before she got her bicycle,
She sometimes used to make
The beds and wash the dishes,
And help her mother bake.
But now she's got her bicycle,
She doesn't do a thing
About the house, but day and night
She's always on the wing!

An
American
Girls
Pastime

START A
BICYCLE CLUB

*Get your friends together
to play bicycle games!*

When Samantha was a girl, a bicycling
craze was sweeping America. Almost
every town had a bicycling club. The clubs
organized bike tours and parades, as well
as games such as "ten-pin rides," in which
bicyclists rode in and out of a row of bowling pins.

Get a group of your friends together
to form a bicycle club. Choose a name and
a place to meet, then play some fun games
on your bicycles!

Organize Your Bicycle Club

Invite your friends to a bicycle club kickoff. A *kickoff* is a time for planning and organizing. At your club kickoff, you'll want to choose the following:

1. *A club name.* Give your bicycle club a name with a personal touch. You might want to name it after your town, such as "The Baltimore Bicycle Club." Be sure the name describes all of the club members.

2. *When and where to meet.* Many clubs meet once a week or every other week. You might decide to meet more often in the summer than in the winter. Then choose a meeting place. You may be able to meet at one member's house or take turns meeting at different members' houses. Or meet at a park or playground that's close to everyone.

3. *Club activities.* What will you do at your meetings? Turn the page for some great ideas!

Important: Be sure to follow these safety rules when playing bicycle games:
- *Play the games only during daylight.*
- *Wear a helmet.*
- *Ride where there is no car traffic, such as in a backyard, playground, or park.*

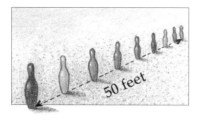

50 feet

Ten-Pin Rides

Mark start and finish lines about 50 feet apart. In between the lines, set up obstacles such as plastic bowling pins, tin cans, or milk jugs. Place the obstacles in a straight line. The closer the obstacles are to one another, the harder the course will be.

Each rider takes a turn weaving around the obstacles from start to finish. Another player uses a watch with a

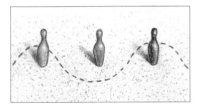

second hand to time the rider. If the rider touches an obstacle, 1 second is added to her total time. If she knocks over an obstacle, 2 seconds are added. If she skips an obstacle, 3 seconds are added. The rider with the fastest time wins.

Beanbag Balance

Samantha had to practice perfect posture when she walked. She might have had to when she bicycled, too!

All the riders balance beanbags on their helmets and get on their bikes. On "Go!" everyone starts moving. Riders may

 move in any direction and pattern—in circles, straight lines, or figure

eights—but they must not stop. The one who keeps riding *and* keeps the beanbag on her head for the longest time wins.

Riding Relay

Mark a start line and a turnaround line about 50 feet apart. Place 2 pins or cans on the turnaround line about 15 feet apart.

Riders divide into 2 teams and form 2 lines at the start line. Each team has one bike. On "Go!"

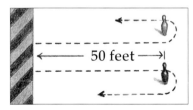

the first rider in each line mounts the bike, pedals to the turnaround line, rounds her team's pin, and rides back to the start line. Then she gives the bike to the next rider on her team. The first team to finish the relay wins!

Bicycle Un-Race

Mark start and finish lines about 30 feet apart. All of the riders line up at the starting line. On "Go!" riders pedal very . . . very . . . slowly toward the finish line. The riders can't touch the ground with their feet, and they must keep going forward. The last one to reach the finish line is the winner.

PO BOX 620497
MIDDLETON WI 53562-0497

American Girl ®

Catalogue Request

Join our mailing list! Just drop this card
in the mail, call **1-800-845-0005**, or visit

or

Due to a printing error, this card
does not meet postal regulations.

Send me a catalogue:

To receive your FREE
American Girl® catalogue,
please call 1-800-845-0005.

Name _____

Address _____

City _____ State _____ Zip 1225i

Girl's birth date: _____ / _____ / _____
          month day year   E-mail _____

Parent's signature _____